كُلُ أَلُوانِ الأَرْضُ
All the Colours of the Earth

SHEILA HAMANAKA

MANTRA   LONDON

Arabic Translation by Sonia El Nimr

First published in 1994 by William Morrow and Company Inc.,
1350 Avenue of the Americas, New York, NY 10019.

Mantra Publishing Ltd
5 Alexandra Grove
London N12 8NU

To Suzy and Kiyo and all the other children of the earth

يَأْتِي الْأَطْفَالُ بِكُلِّ أَلْوَانِ الْأَرْضِ –

Children come in all the colours of the earth -

يَزْخَرُ البَرِّ الدُّبَبَةِ البُنِيّ وَالنُّسُورِ المُحَلِّقَةِ،

The roaring browns of bears and soaring eagles,

بِالـلَّونِ الـذَّهـبِيّ الـهـامِسِ لِحَشـائِشِ نِـهـايـةِ الصَّيـفِ،

The whispering golds of late summer grasses,

والخَمْرِيُّ المُتكَسِّرِ لأوراقِ الشَجَرِ المُتشــــــاقطةِ؛

And crackling russets of fallen leaves,

بـالرَّنـيـنِ الزَّهـرِيِّ لِلْأَصْدافِ الصَّغِيرةِ عـلى
شـاطِـئُ بَحـرٍ صاخِبٍ

The tinkling pinks of tiny seashells
by the rumbling sea.

يَأْتِي الأَطْفَالُ بِشَعْرٍ كَالحِمْلانِ المُتَوَثِّبَةِ

Children come with hair like bouncy baby lambs,

أُوِبشَعْرٍ يَنْسَابُ كَالماء،

Or hair that flows like water,

مِنْ مُلْتَفٍّ كَالْقِطَطِ النَّائِمَةِ بِأَلْوَانِهَا النَّاعِسَةِ

Or hair that curls like sleeping cats in snoozy cat colours.

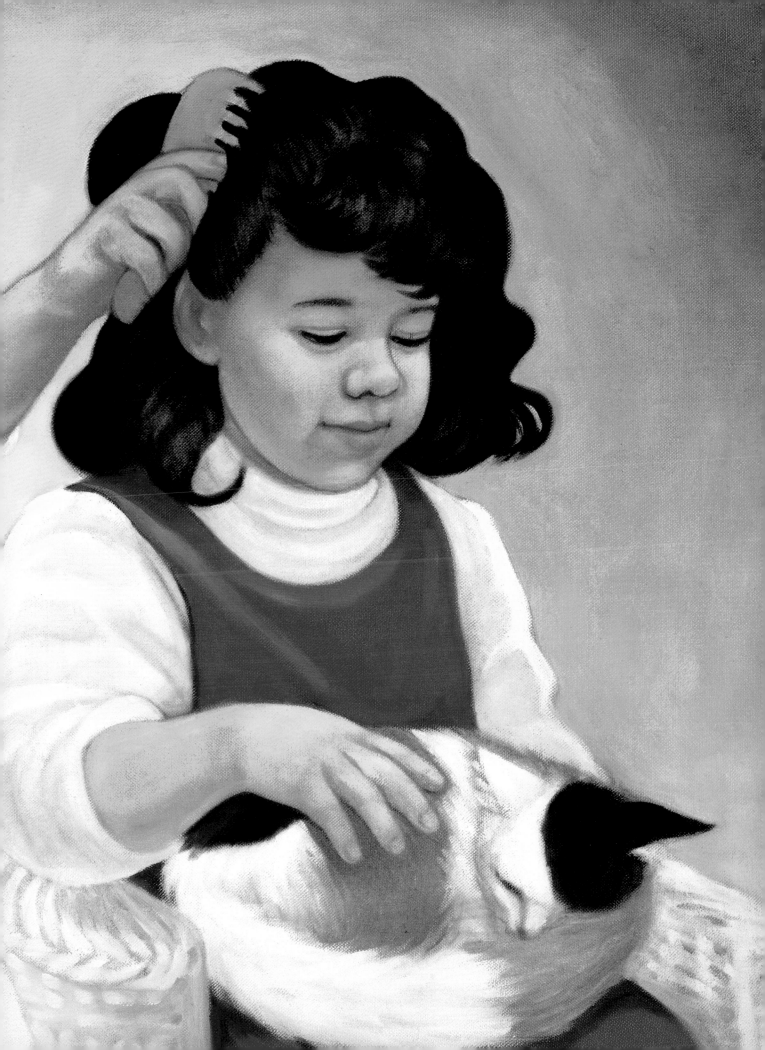

يَأتِي الأطفالُ بِكُلِّ أَلْوانِ الحُبِّ،

Children come in all the colours of love,

بِكُلِّ التَنَوعِ اللامُتناهي لِلَوني وَلَونُكْ.
In endless shades of you and me.

فالحُبُّ يأتي بِلَونِ القِرفَةِ،
وَالجَوزِ، والحِنْطَةِ،

For love comes in cinnamon,
walnut, and wheat,

الحُبُّ عَنْبَرٌ وَعاجٌ وَزَنْجَبيلٌ وَحَلوى
Love is amber and ivory and ginger and sweet

كَالكَراميلِ وَالشوكولاطةِ وَعَسَلِ النَّحْلِ.

Like caramel, and chocolate, and the honey of bees.

داكِنٌ كَبُقَعِ جِلْدِ النَّمِرِ، وفاتِحٌ كالرَّمْلِ،

Dark as leopard spots, light as sand,

الأطفالُ بِضَحِكاتِهِمْ الرَّنانةِ التي تُقَبِّلُ أَرْضَنا،

Children buzz with laughter that kisses our land,

بِأَشِعَّةِ الشَّمسِ، سُعَداءَ وَطُلَقاءَ كَالفَراشاتِ،

With sunlight like butterflies happy and free,

يَأْتِي الأَطْفالُ بِكُلِّ أَلْوانِ الأَرْضِ
وَالبَحْرِ وَالسَّماءُ ۔

Children come in all the colours
of the earth and sky and sea.